An Easter Surprise

The Tale of LINDT GOLD BUNNY

by the Lindt Master Chocolatier

Peter E. Randall Publisher
Portsmouth, New Hampshire
2016

It was the day before Easter. I was in my kitchen, mixing hot chocolate, looking out the window. My neighbors were outside enjoying the bright spring day. Birds were calling and the daffodils smiled in the sun.

I saw Mia laughing and running through her yard, chasing a butterfly. She stopped suddenly and crouched near a lilac bush.

I wondered, *Now what does she see?*

I stepped outside to get a closer look. There was a golden-haired bunny sitting right in front of her! Mia reached out to touch its soft fur, but the bunny jumped and ran away.

Mia cried out, "The bunny! It ran away!"
She burst into tears.

Her big brother Josh put his arm
around her, "You okay, Sis?"

I decided to help her, too.

"Don't worry, Mia," I said. "I bet your bunny didn't go far."

"It's the Master Chocolatier!" she said, smiling through her tears. "Do you know about bunnies?"

"I've seen them right over there," I said, pointing at the bike path and green space running behind the yards.

"Me too!" said Josh. "They live in between the trees and under the bushes. I read that bunnies like places where they can feel safe."

"But I want a bunny that will stay!" said Mia, as her father picked her up for a hug.

Hmmm... I was thinking... *A bunny that will stay...* I was getting one of my great ideas.

"I think I know a way to help the bunnies feel safe in our yard," said her mom.

"What way?" asked Mia.

"We can build a bunny nest!" said her mom.

"A what?" said Mia and Josh.

"A bunny nest! It's a place where bunnies can feel cozy and safe when they visit us," she said, pulling them in for a double hug.

"Look! We can build it at the back of the yard where it's green," said their dad. "These sticks I cut from the bushes will make a perfect bunny nest!"

"Can we get sticks from your yard, too?" Josh asked me.

"I like the way you think!" I said with a laugh.

Mia and Josh started gathering sticks. Their mom piled more into the wheelbarrow. They all began to build a bunny nest at the back of their yard.

I've got a great idea! I thought, as I headed back to my house. *This will be the best Easter surprise ever!*

I just had to get to my BIG kitchen.

I went to my BIG kitchen.
I opened my huge cupboard and checked my giant refrigerator. I snapped on the island light and began to take out bowls, spoons, and whisks—all my favorite chocolate-making tools.

As I took out all the ingredients for my Easter surprise, I thought of Mia's family. I hoped they were having fun building a safe place for bunnies.

And now I was going to make sure Mia had a bunny that would stay.

I measured the cocoa.
I measured the sugar. I
measured the milk. I had to
get the mixture just right.
Easter was coming, so
I had to work fast!

I mixed and stirred and poured the chocolate into a perfect confection. The sweet chocolate scent floated up, swirled around, and filled my BIG kitchen with Easter magic.

Finally, I had the melted chocolate just right. It smelled delicious!

Using my tools, I began to shape a new mold for this rich treat. When it was perfect, I poured in the chocolate...

It was almost dawn when the chocolate had cooled. I thought about the glowing fur on Mia's bunny. I got down my gold foil and wrapped my Easter surprises. Then I went to put my tools away and tidy up.

When I returned, I found the Easter surprises were gone! "I bet I know who took those!" I said, smiling to myself.

The sun was wide awake when I got back home. Since it was Easter morning, there were already eggs and other treasures hidden all over the neighborhood!

"Hello!" I said as I waved to my neighbors. They were sipping hot chocolate in the back yard.

"Happy Easter!" they called, waving me over.

I had just joined them for a hot chocolate when suddenly the children came bursting through the back door!

It was an epic Easter egg hunt! Mia squealed at all the goodies hidden in the yard. Josh shouted and swung his basket as he ran around the yard, finding lots of eggs.

There were treats in the garden, treats in the tulips, treats under the picnic table. Josh even found a chocolate egg in a birdhouse!

"Master Chocolatier!" called Josh. "The Easter Bunny's been here!"
"But where is it now?" said Mia. "Where has that bunny gone?"
"Well, where does a bunny feel safe?" asked her mom.

"Think about it," said her dad, as he tousled her hair. Suddenly Mia knew where to find a bunny.

She ran to the bunny nest with Josh and their friends close behind. She got down on her knees and looked inside...

"It's a Gold Bunny!" she whispered. "And look! TWO BUNNIES!"

"Where?" said Josh, looking over her shoulder.
"Shhh..." said Mia, pointing. Then they all saw it.
"Wow!" he said. "It's like we have our own Easter Bunny."

Mia picked up the basket and slowly moved back so she wouldn't frighten the real bunny. She danced across the yard with her friends, calling out, "Master Chocolatier! Look at what I found!"

Her smile was a mile wide as Mia proudly held up the basket with Gold Bunny, declaring, "Now I have a bunny that will stay. This is the best Easter surprise ever!"

The Master Chocolatiers at Lindt have perfected the art of creating the finest chocolate, which requires great skill and passion.

For over 170 years, they have been developing innovative chocolate recipes with meticulous craftsmanship, resulting in superior-tasting, premium chocolate.

The Lindt GOLD BUNNY, created by the Lindt Master Chocolatier and wrapped in golden foil with a red ribbon, is a worldwide symbol of Easter that continues to delight everyone's inner child.

Produced by Peter E. Randall Publisher
ISBN 978-0-692-51521-1

Printed in Canada